i A
n T
t I
a S
p N
s P

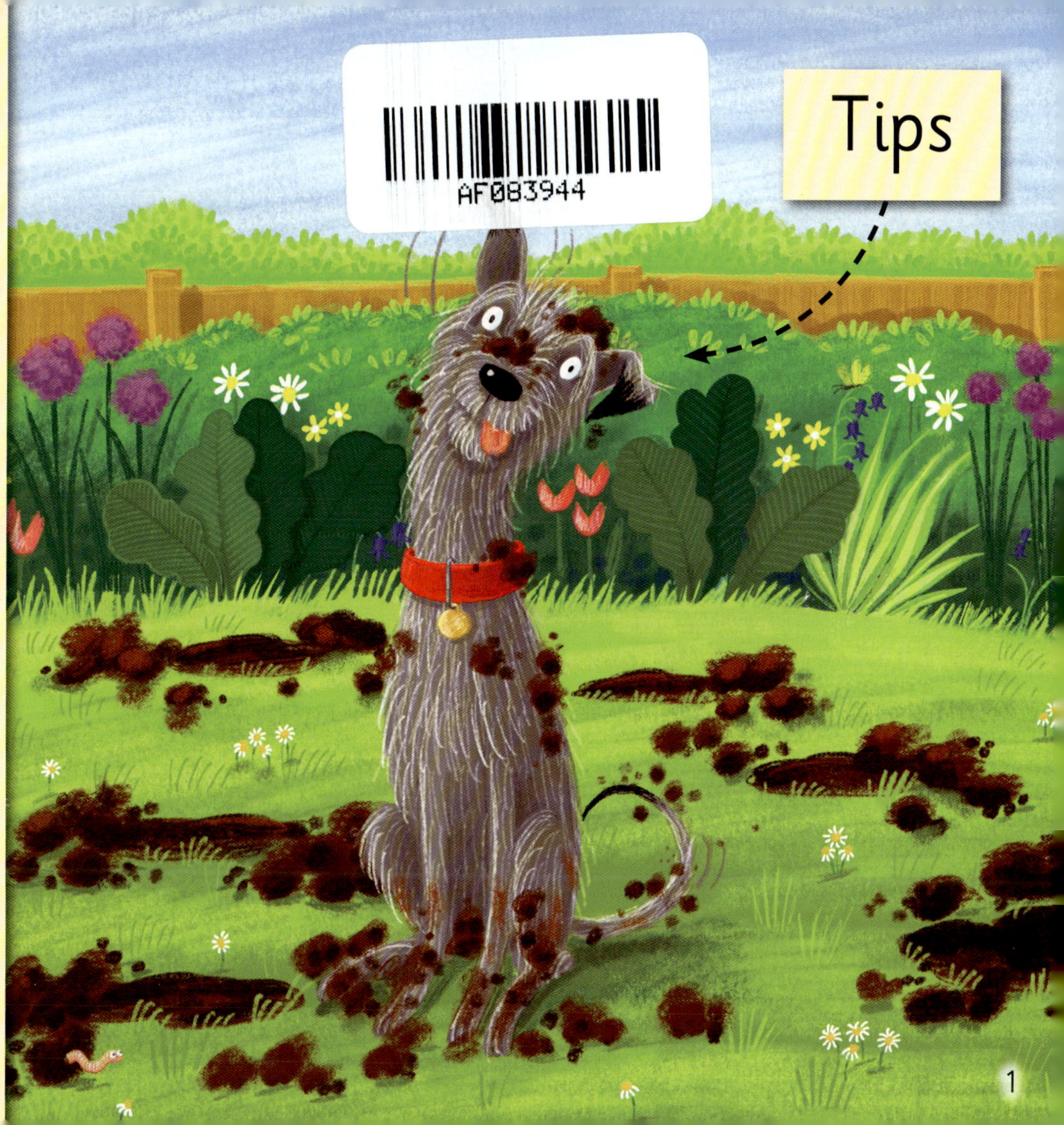

AF083944

Pat

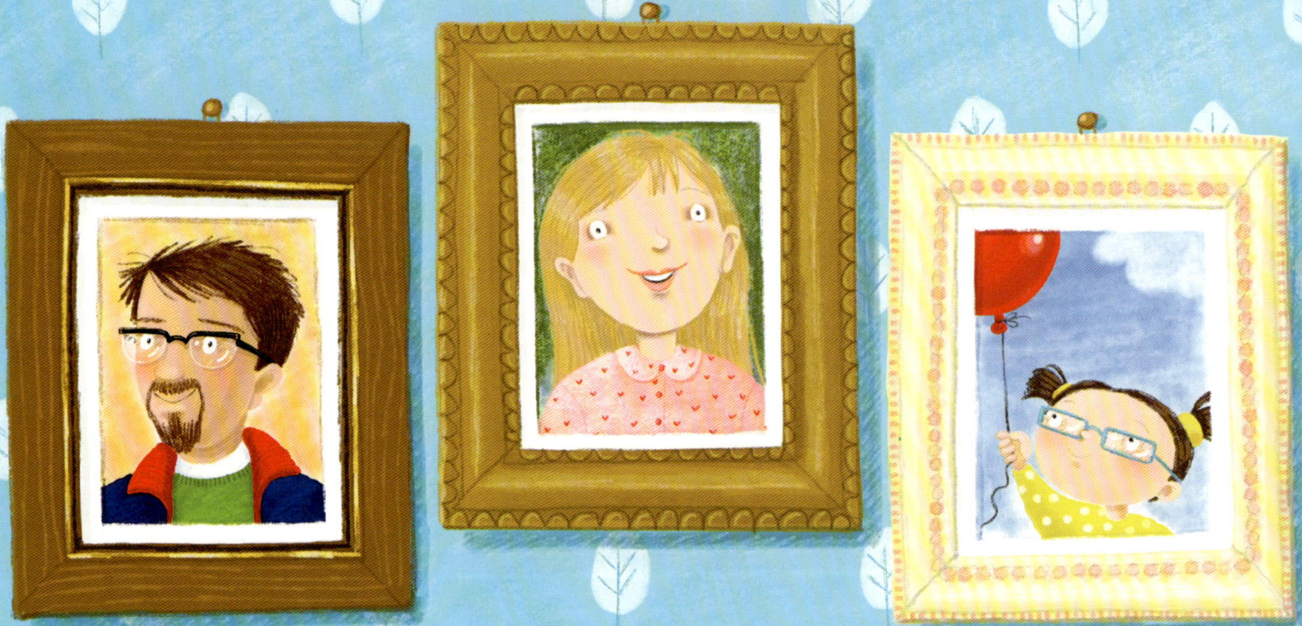

Stan

Pip

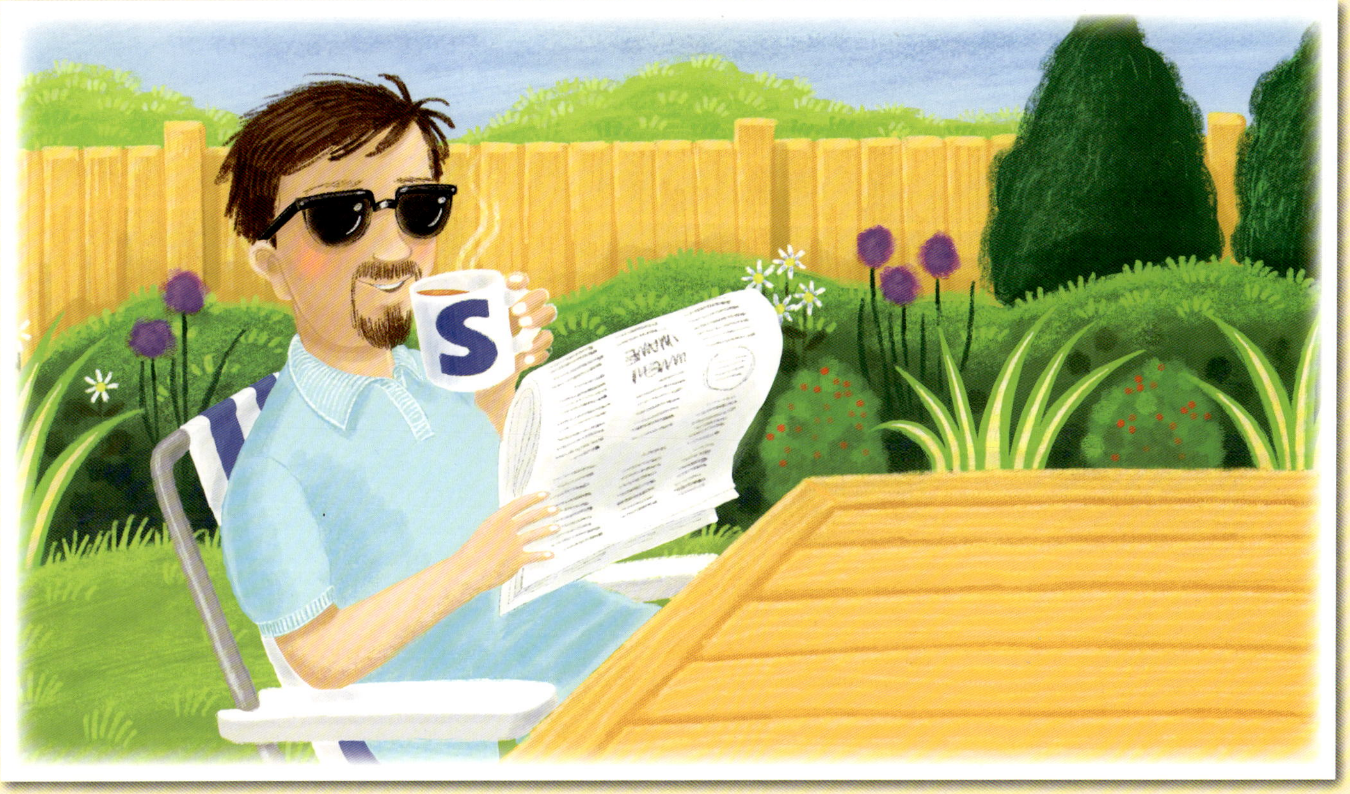

Stan sips.

Pat naps.

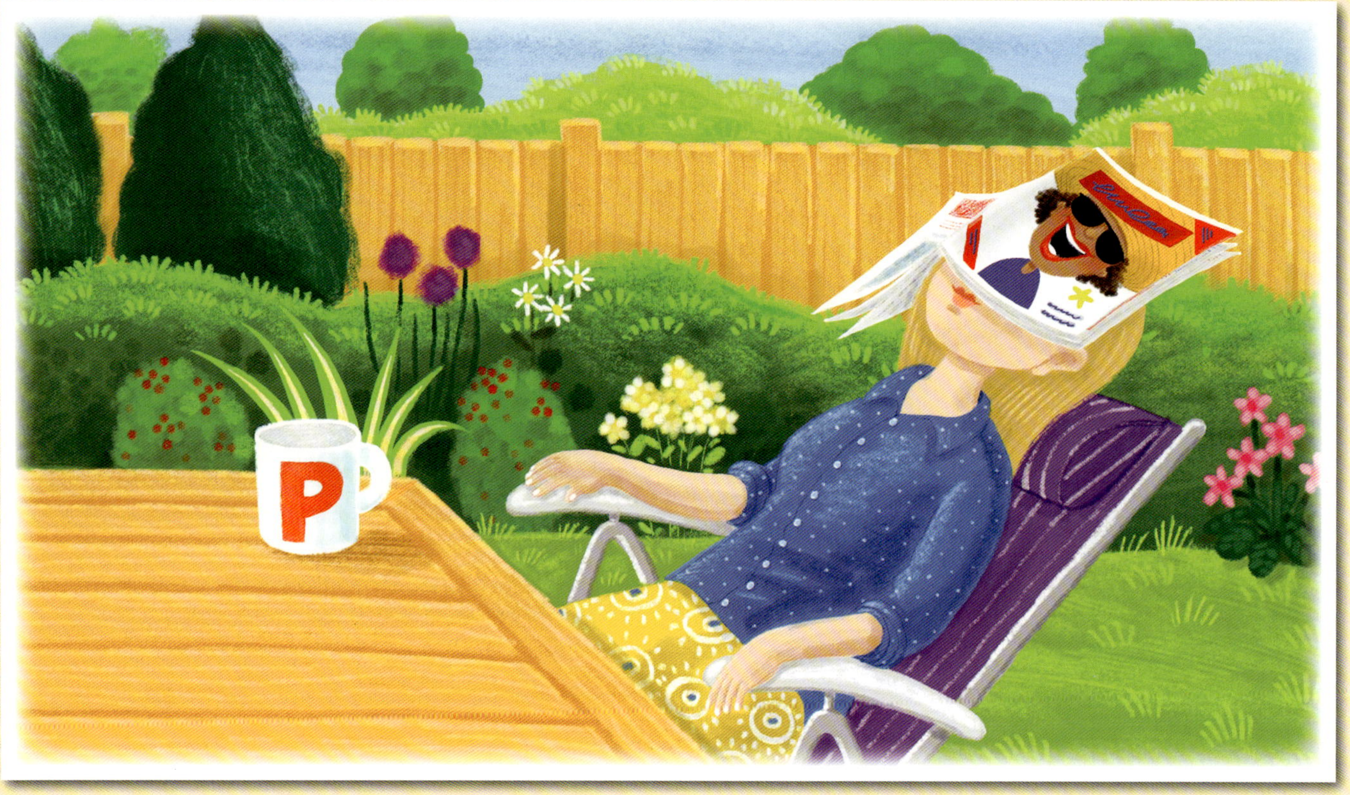

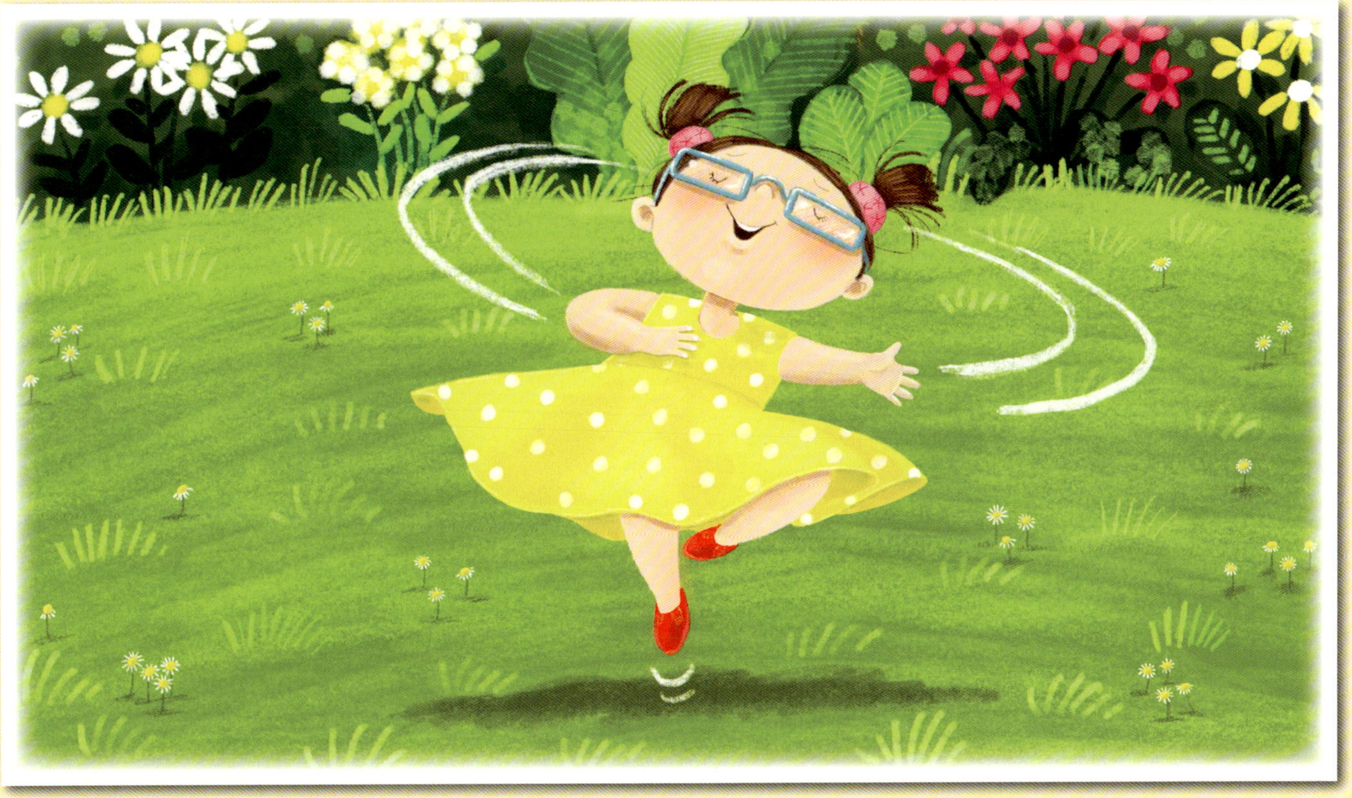

Pip spins.

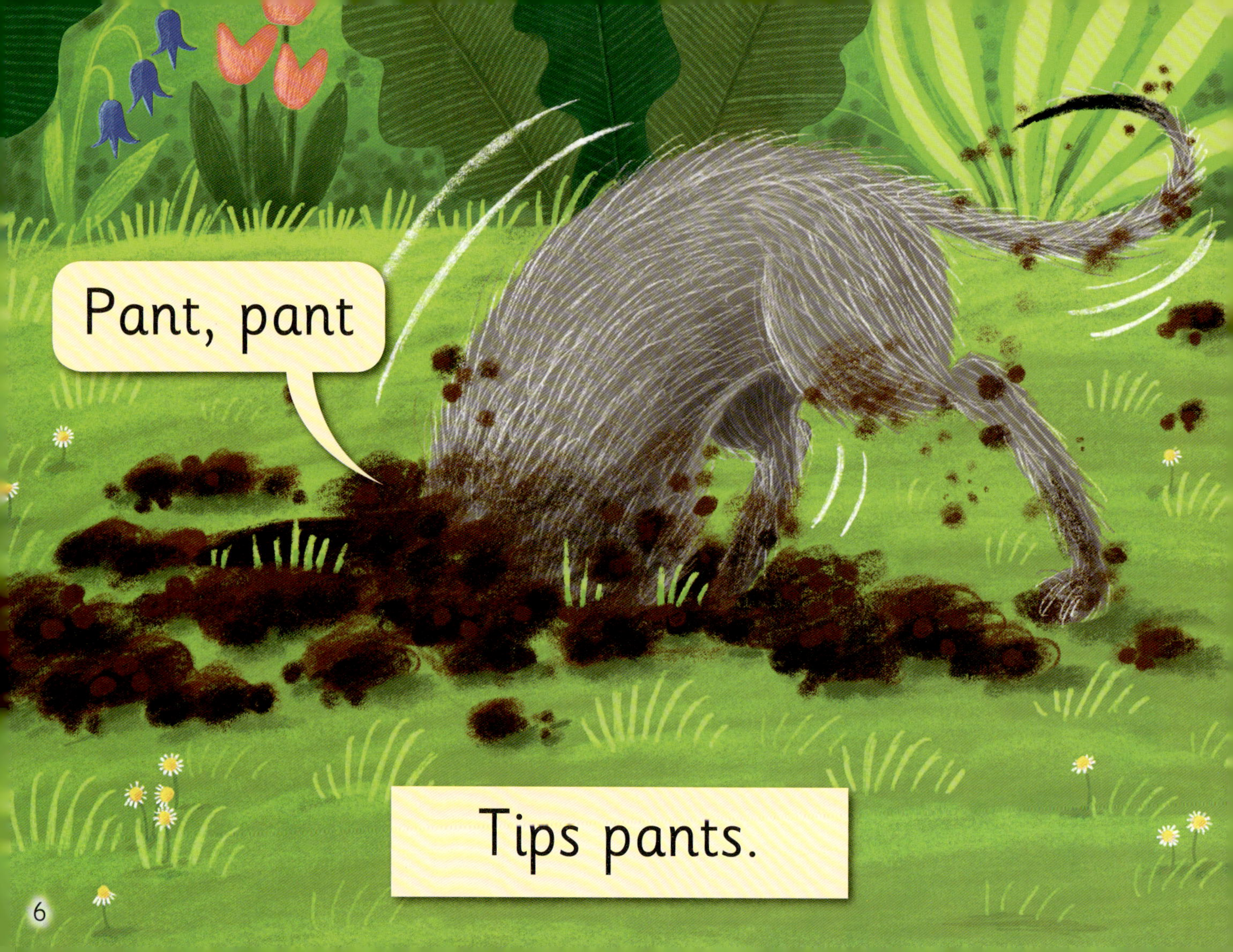

Tips pants.

Tips sits in a pit.

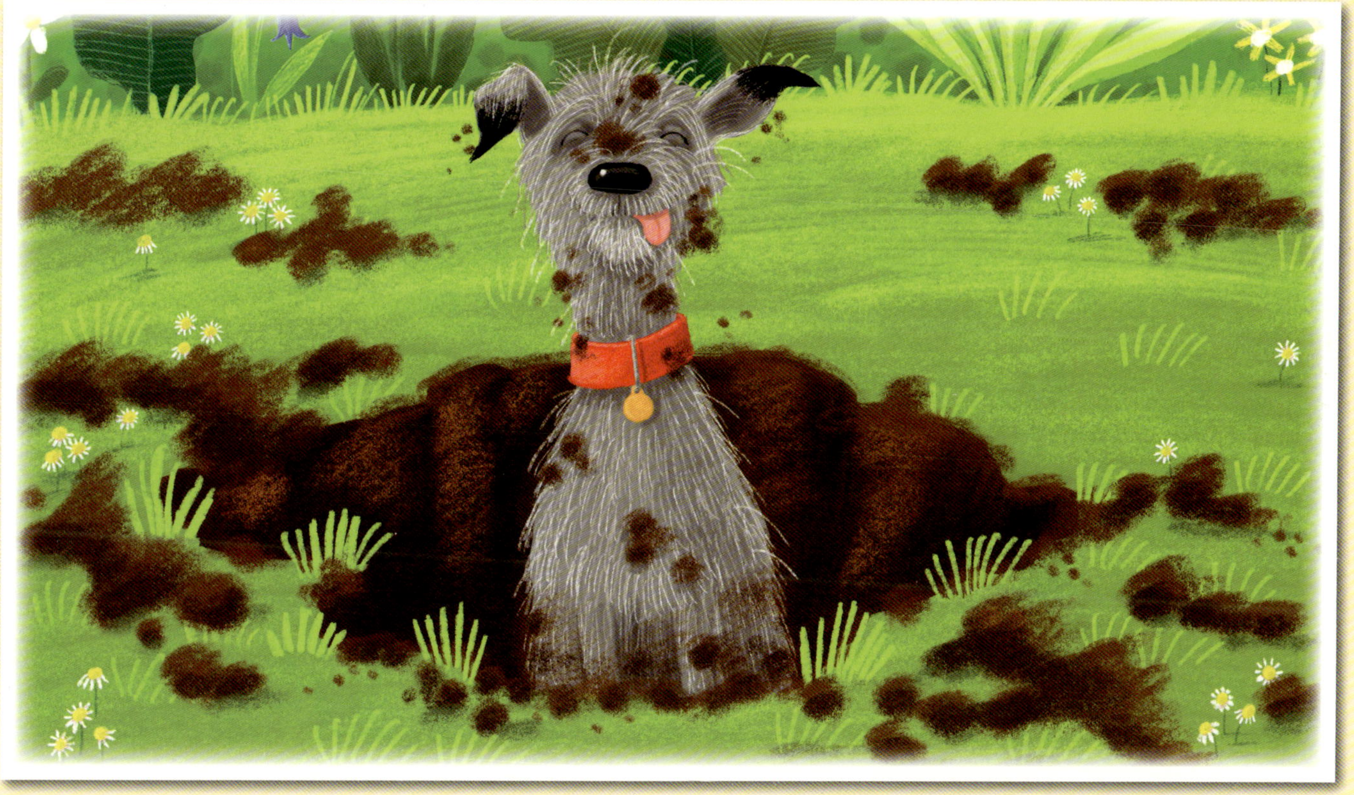

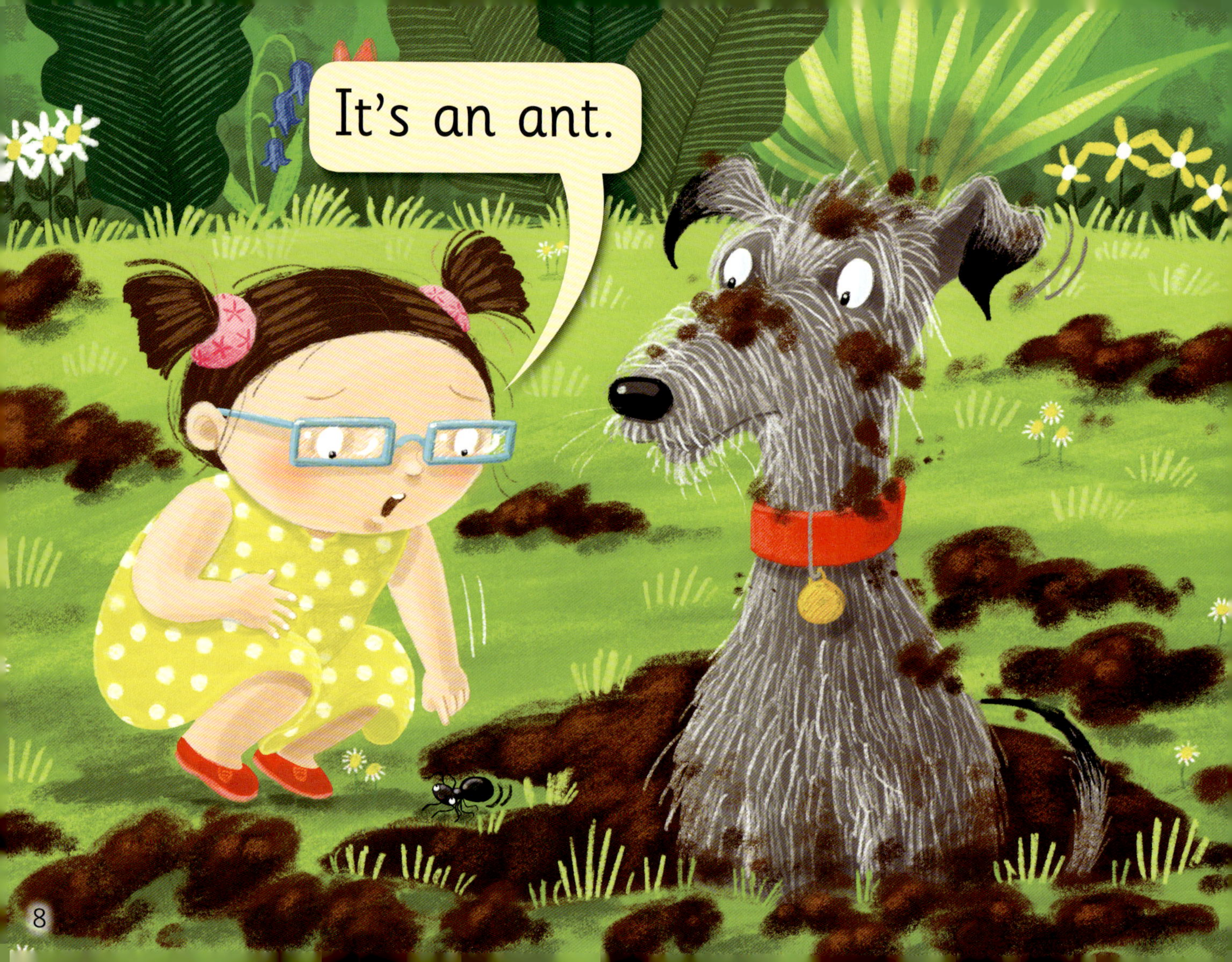
It's an ant.

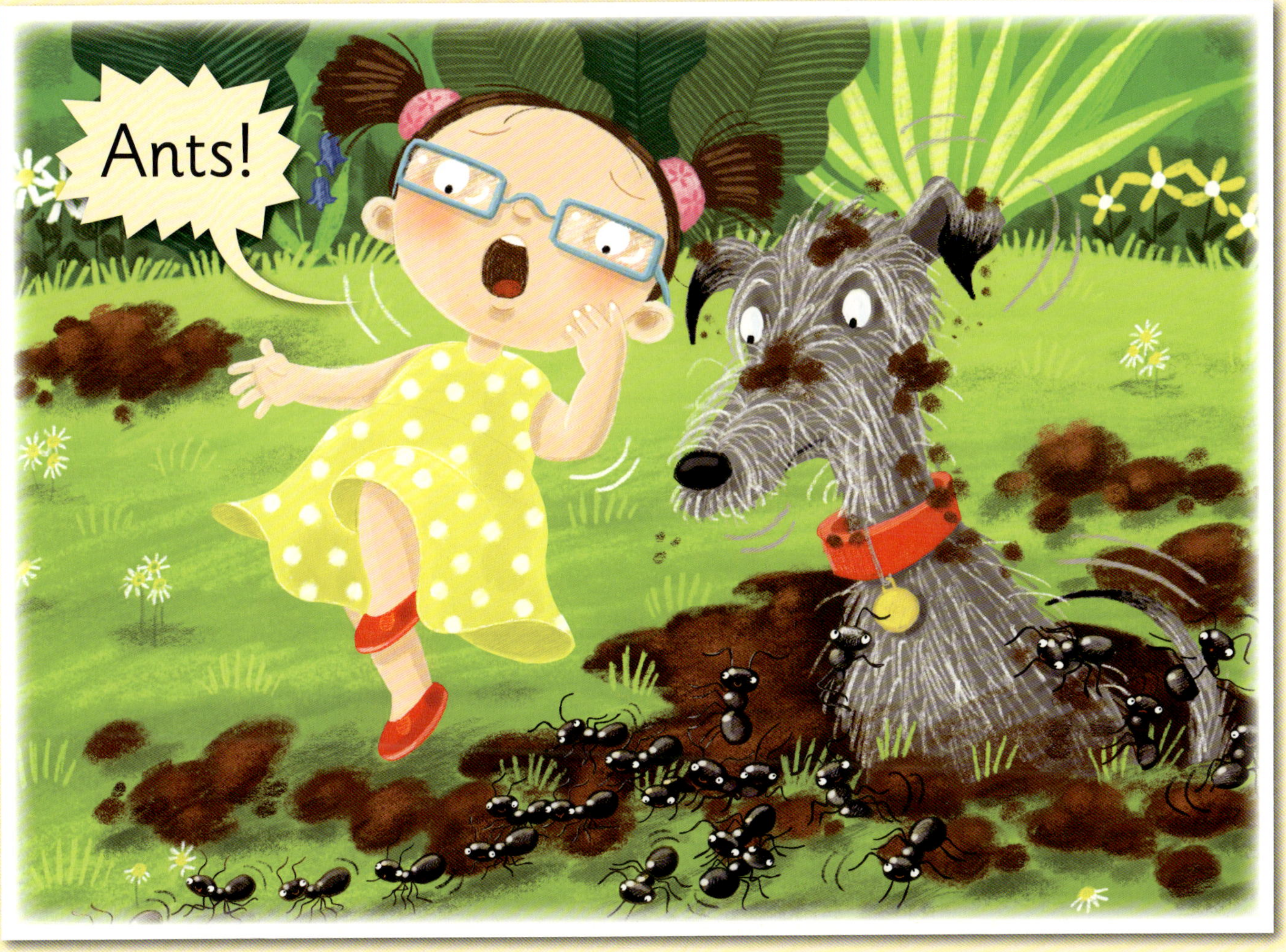
Ants!

Ants nip at Tips.

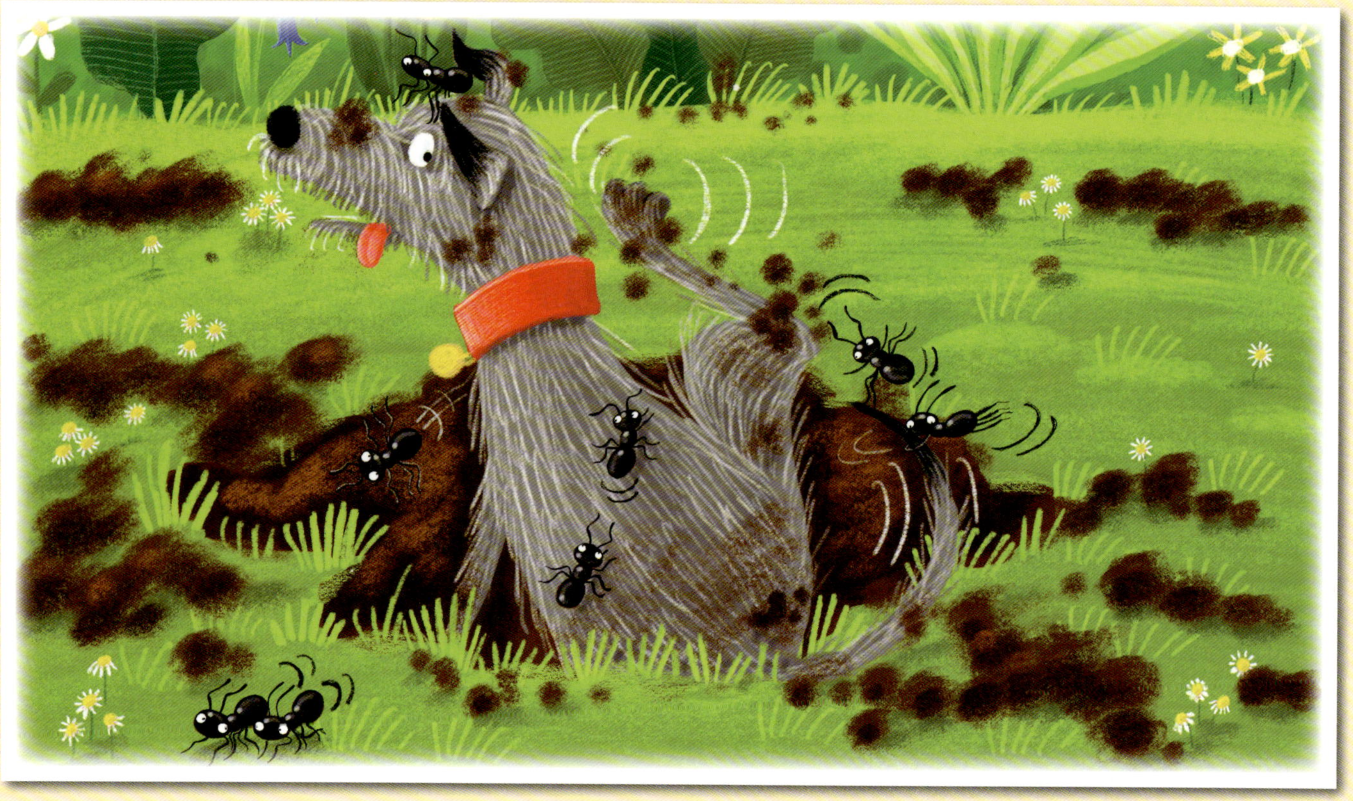

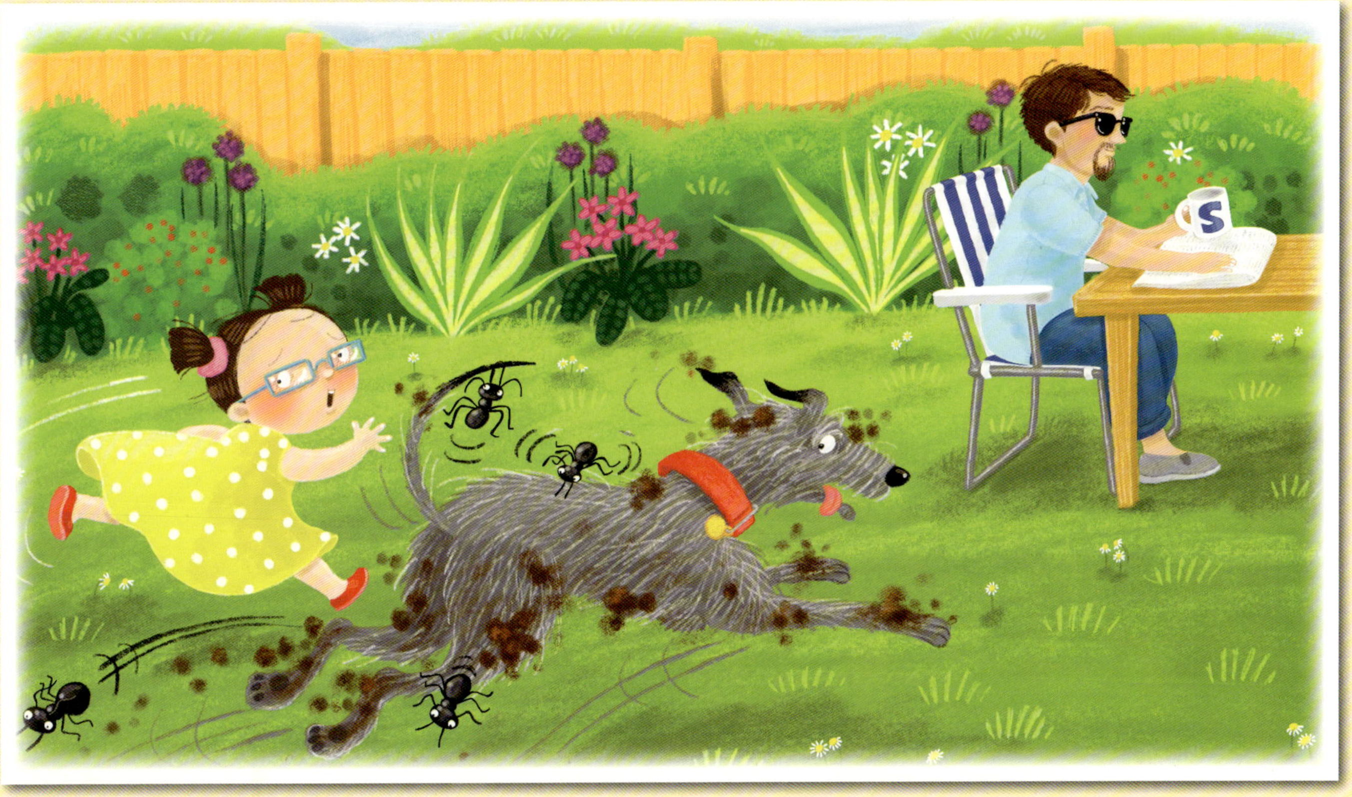

Pant, pant, pant.

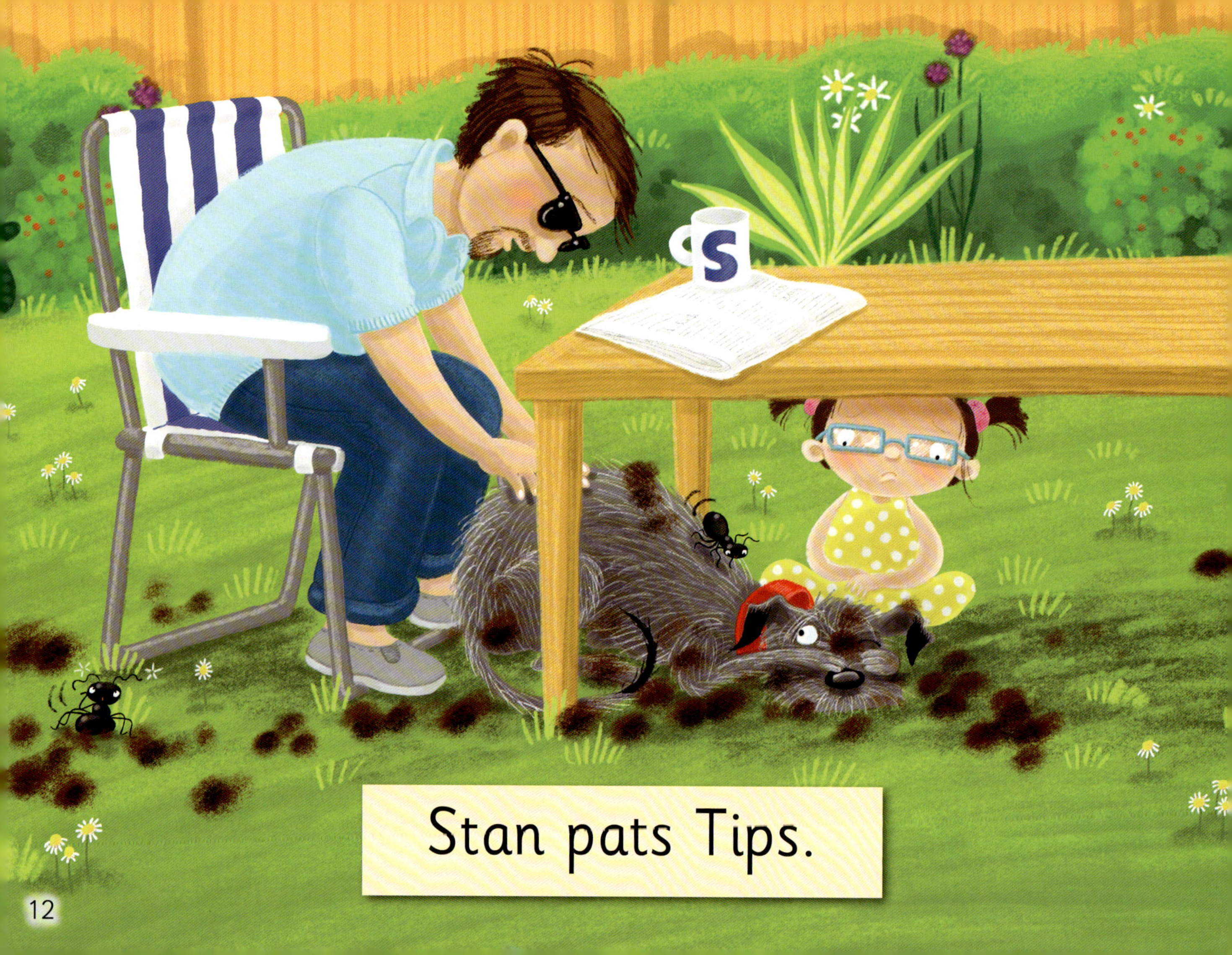

Stan pats Tips.